MONSTER BROTHER

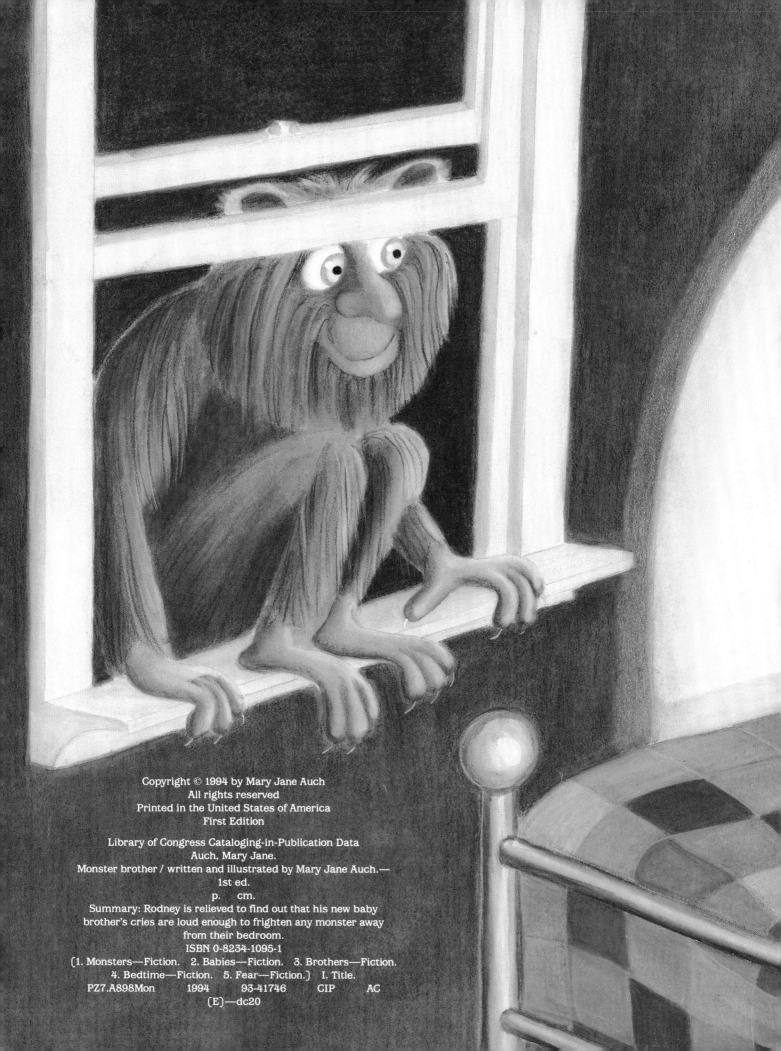

Library of Congress Cataloging-in-Publication Data
Auch, Mary Jane.
Monster brother / written and illustrated by Mary Jane Auch.—
1st ed.
p.   cm.
Summary: Rodney is relieved to find out that his new baby
brother's cries are loud enough to frighten any monster away
from their bedroom.
ISBN 0-8234-1095-1
(1. Monsters—Fiction.   2. Babies—Fiction.   3. Brothers—Fiction.
4. Bedtime—Fiction.   5. Fear—Fiction.)   I. Title.
PZ7.A898Mon   1994   93-41746   CIP   AC
(E)—dc20

MONSTER BROTHER

written and illustrated by
Mary Jane Auch

Holiday House/New York

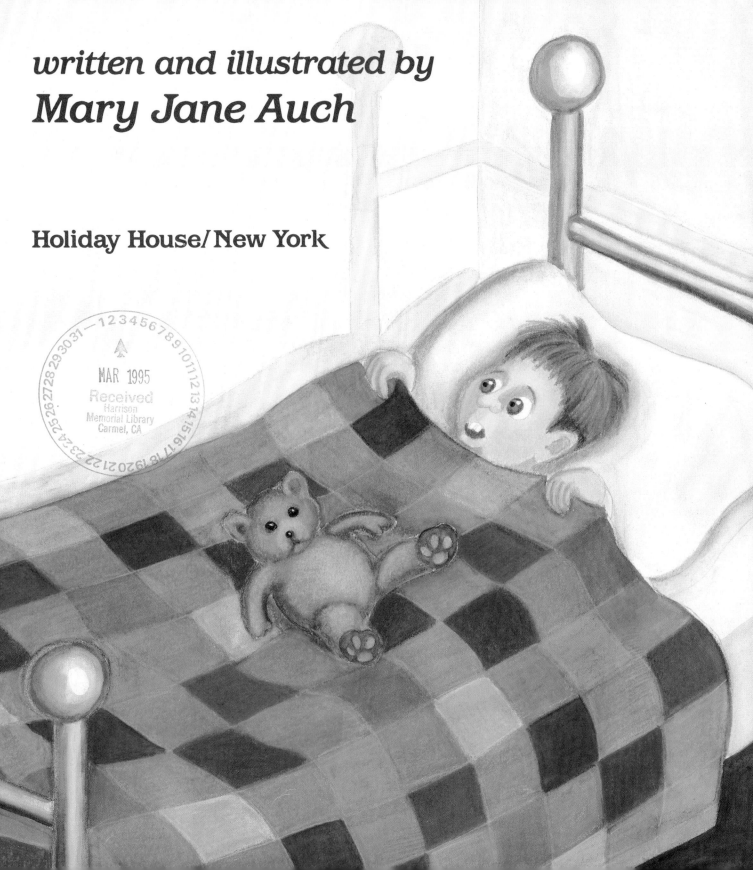

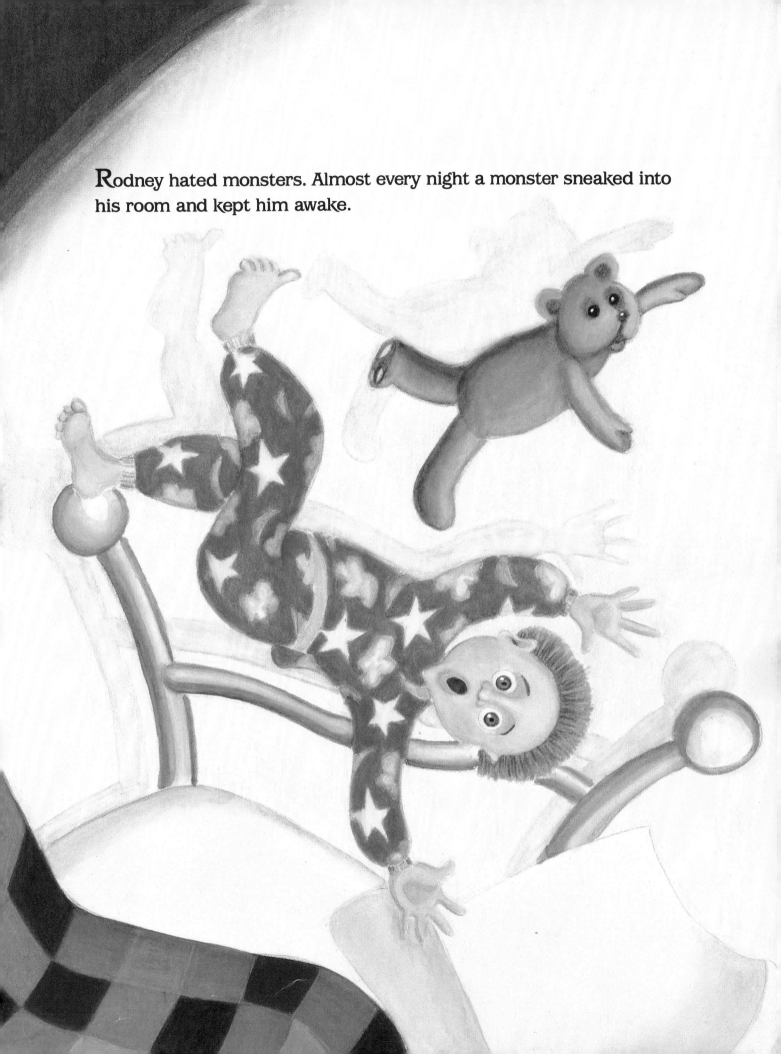

Rodney hated monsters. Almost every night a monster sneaked into his room and kept him awake.

"The monsters always wait until dark," Rodney told his mother. "Let's make my room lighter, so they'll stay away."

"Good idea," said Rodney's mother. That night they put lots of extra lights in Rodney's room, but a monster came anyway.

He was wearing sunglasses!

Now Rodney couldn't sleep because his room was too bright, so his mother got rid of all the extra lights.

"I have another idea," said Rodney. "I bet the monsters would stay away if my room smelled bad."

"Good idea," said Rodney's father. He put a hunk of stinky cheese on Rodney's bed, but that night a monster came anyway.

He was wearing a clothespin on his nose!

"The room needs to be smellier," said Rodney, so on the bed they added a dead catfish, an old pair of sneakers, some rotten eggs, and even a pair of gym socks that hadn't been washed for six months!

But the monsters kept coming.
Now Rodney couldn't sleep because
his room smelled terrible, so his
daddy took away all the stinky
things.

The next night at bedtime, Rodney's mother had a surprise. "Guess what? Mommy's going to bring home a baby brother for you. Isn't that exciting?"

"No, thanks," said Rodney. "I don't need a baby brother."

"But then you'll have someone to play with," said Mommy. "Won't that be fun?"

"Playing with you and Daddy is fun," said Rodney. "I don't *want* a baby brother."

"With a baby brother, you won't have to sleep in your room alone," said Mommy.

That gave Rodney an idea. A monster would think twice about going into a room with *two* kids in it. "Okay, I'll try a baby brother," Rodney said. "Bring one home."

"The baby will come this summer," said Mommy, "soon after Aunt Celeste's wedding."

In the next few months,
Rodney helped Mommy get
ready for his new brother.

Every night he dreamed a monster came to his room, but when it saw two kids, it ran away. Rodney could hardly wait until his brother arrived.

"Who will the baby look like?"
Rodney asked his mommy one day. She
brought out a scrapbook and showed
Rodney all of his baby pictures. "He
might look like you," she said. "We'll
have to wait and see."

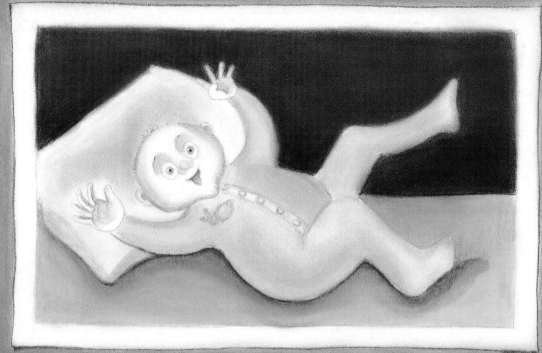

RODNEY SAYS, "GOOD MORNING, MOMMY!"

WHERE'S MY FOOD?

WATCH ME DANCE!

Finally it was the day of Aunt Celeste's wedding.

"Is the baby coming today?" asked Rodney.

"I hope not," said Mommy. "But he'll be here soon."

All the relatives at the wedding were talking about the baby.

"I wonder who your new brother will look like?" said Grandma. "Maybe he'll get my big blue eyes."

"I hope the baby gets my distinguished nose," said Grandpa.

"What if he gets my scrawny chicken legs?" giggled Aunt Velma.

"If he's like cousin Ernie," said Aunt Celeste,
"he'll grow like a weed."

Suddenly, Rodney thought he saw his new brother. "I know what the baby looks like!" he cried, but nobody paid any attention to him. They were too busy smiling for the camera.

"We're all going to know what the baby looks like very soon!" exclaimed Rodney's mommy. "I think he's coming right now."

"Let's tell the baby to go away, Mommy," said Rodney. "I think babies are a very bad idea."

Mommy gave Rodney a hug. "Aunt Velma will stay with you until we come home with the baby. Don't worry, honey. Everything is going to be fine."

But Rodney did worry.
He worried for two whole days.
He worried that the baby would take away all of his toys.
He worried that the baby would eat up all of Grandma's cookies.
Most of all, he worried about . . .

BEING ALONE
IN HIS ROOM
IN THE DARK
WITH **THE BABY!**

"Rodney," called Aunt Velma, "come see the baby."

"I *see* him!" yelled Rodney.

"Mommy and the baby are out here. Come see!"

"Mommy's home?" Rodney ran out of his room.

Mommy was sitting with a small bundle in her arms.

She smiled. "See? Here's your brother, Sidney. He looks just like . . ."

"Me!" Rodney cried. "He looks just like me—only a lot smaller." Rodney loved his brother the minute he saw him.

That night, Rodney watched Sidney fall asleep. "I like having you in my room, Sidney," he whispered. "There's only one problem. You're too little to scare away monsters. But don't worry, I'll protect you."

Rodney took his baseball bat and stood by the open window. "If you monsters dare come near my baby brother," he yelled, "I'll bop you right in the nose. POW!"

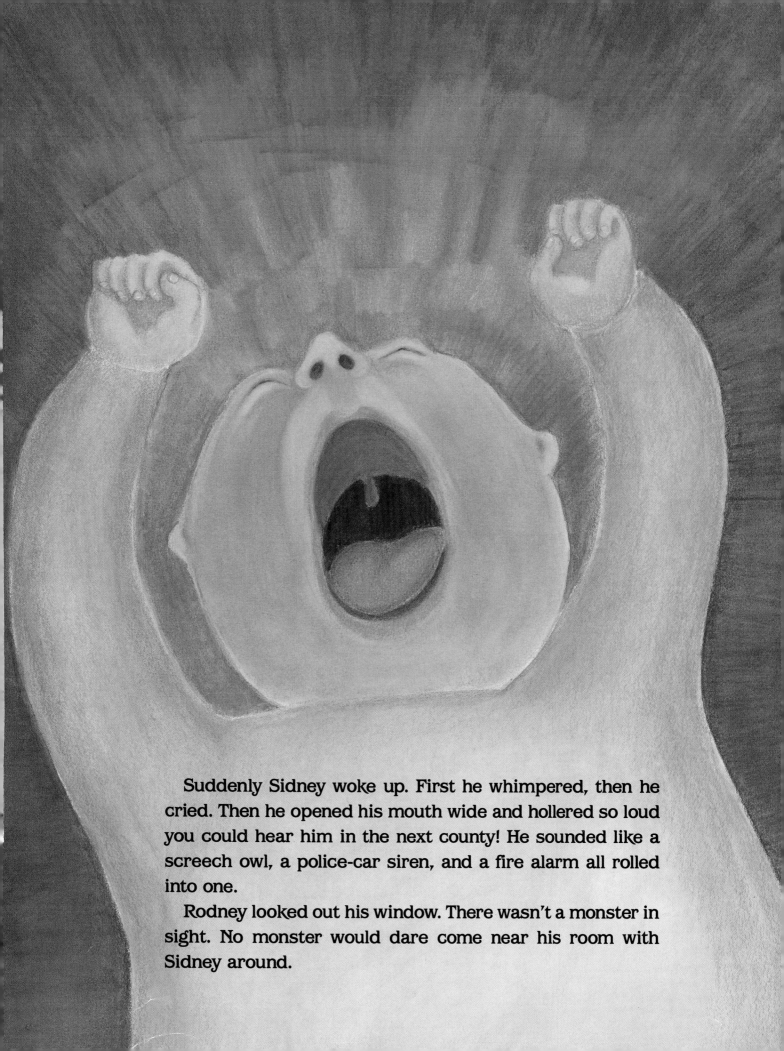

Suddenly Sidney woke up. First he whimpered, then he cried. Then he opened his mouth wide and hollered so loud you could hear him in the next county! He sounded like a screech owl, a police-car siren, and a fire alarm all rolled into one.

Rodney looked out his window. There wasn't a monster in sight. No monster would dare come near his room with Sidney around.

Hooray! The monsters were gone!
And Rodney—finally—could get a good night's sleep.